When This Box Is Full

By
Patricia Lillie

Pictures by
Donald Crews

Greenwillow Books
New York

The black-and-white
photographs were reproduced
from line conversions screened
with a "Lasergrain" pattern.
Color was added by hand with
film overlays. The text type is
Helvetica Black Italic.

Library of Congress
Cataloging-in-Publication Data
Lillie, Patricia.
When this box is full /
by Patricia Lillie;
pictures by Donald Crews.
        p.   cm.
Summary: Each month a child
adds something to an empty
box, including a red foil heart in
February and toasted pumpkin
seeds in October.
ISBN 0-688-12016-4 (trade).
ISBN 0-688-12017-2 (lib. bdg.)
[1. Months—fiction.]
I. Crews, Donald, ill.
II. Title.
PZ7.L632Wi   1993
[E]—dc20
92-28743   CIP   AC

Endpaper boxes
from Donald Crews's
private collection

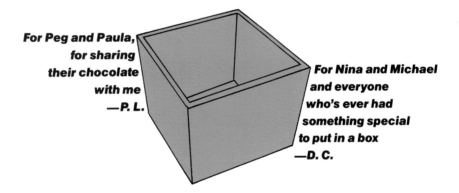

This box
is empty...
but not
for long.

I will fill
it with...

January

a snowman's scarf,

January
February
March

a red
foil heart,

a robin's
feather,

January
February
March
April

a purple
eggshell,

January
February
March
April
May
June

a wild
daisy,

**helicopters
from the
maple tree,**

January

February

March

April

May

June

July

**a seashell
and some
sand,**

January

February

March

April

May

June

July

August

**a ribbon
from
the fair,**

January

February

March

April

May

June

July

August

September

**a red
leaf,**

January
February
March
April
May
June
July
August
September
October

toasted
pumpkin
seeds,

January
February
March
April
May
June
July
August
September
October
November
December

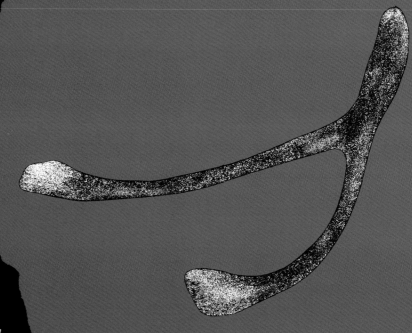

a wishbone,

and
a silver
star.

And then...

I will
share it
with you.